This book
belongs to

....

Puddle's Fan Pages

Here's what other children have to say about their favourite puppy and his latest adventure!

"I liked it when Puddle took them through the puddle and they found the dragon. I'd like to read more books about Puddle. I liked the girls in the story. They had nice names and I think they would be nice friends." Maia, age 5

" I like this book. Puddle is a funny dog - he gets into trouble." Jasmine, age 5

"I liked the character Ruby the best because she holds her plaits for good luck and she was fun. It said the fog was like 'being trapped in a marshmallow' that made me laugh and made me want to be in a marshmallow." Lilly, age 7

Dragon Dance

Other books about
Puddle the Naughtiest Puppy:

Puddle
the naughtiest puppy

Dragon Dance

by Hayley Daze
illustrated by Rowan Clifford
cover illustrated by Paul Hardman

A catalogue record for this book is available from the British Library

Published by Ladybird Books Ltd MMX
A Penguin Company
Penguin Books Ltd., 80 Strand, London WC2R 0RL, UK
Penguin Books Australia Ltd., Camberwell, Victoria, Australia
Penguin Group (NZ) 67 Apollo Drive, Rosedale,
North Shore 0632, New Zealand

1 3 5 7 9 10 8 6 4 2
Series created by Working Partners Limited, London WC1X 9HH
Text © Working Partners Ltd MMX
Cover illustration © Working Partners Ltd MMX
Interior illustrations © Ladybird Books Ltd MMX

Special thanks to Mo O'Hara

ISBN: 978-1-40930-331-2
Printed in England

Mixed Sources

Product group from well-managed
forests and other controlled sources
www.fsc.org   Cert no. SA-COC-001592
© 1996 Forest Stewardship Council

FSC

For Victoria
Wishing you a lifetime of magical adventures

When clouds fill the sky and rain starts to fall,
Ruby and Harry are not sad at all.
They know that when puddles appear on the ground,
A magical puppy will soon be around!

Puddle's his name, and he's the one
Who can lead you to worlds of adventure and fun!
He may be quite naughty, but he's clever too,
So come follow Puddle – he's waiting for you!

A present from Puddle:

Look out for the special code at the back of the book to
get extra-special games and loads of free stuff at Puddle's
website! Come and play at www.puddlethepuppy.com

Contents

Chapter One
Flying High

"Ready for blast-off," Ruby shouted. She held a string that stretched all the way across Grandad's garden. "In five, four, three, two . . ."

"Wait!" Her cousin Harry interrupted the countdown. He was holding a diamond-shaped kite that was attached to Ruby's long string. "There's just one more thing that I want to fix."

Grandad had showed them how he had made kites when he was a child. The cousins had spent all morning making a kite of their own. Ruby

and Harry had used some Christmas
wrapping, some tissue paper that
Ruby thought matched her leggings,
some comic-book pages, wool and
lots of *Well Done* stickers that Harry
had saved from school.

"I want to adjust the tail so it gives
us more drag," Harry called, as he
pushed his glasses back into place.

"I don't want the tail to drag," Ruby
said. "That'll ruin all the bows I've
tied to it."

"I don't mean drag on the ground –
I mean drag as in thrust, lift and drag.
They are the forces that make the kite
fly," Harry explained.

"Come on, Harry. It's not rocket

science," Ruby teased.

"But it is rocket science . . . Oh, never mind," Harry said as he worked on the tail. "Hey, did you know that kites were first made in China over two thousand years ago? They made flying dragons and giant birds –"

"I wish I could fly like a kite," Ruby squealed as she spread her cardigan

out like a cape and pretended to soar around the garden.

"I don't think you'll fly," Harry said, putting the final touches to the kite's tail, "but this will."

"Hooray," Ruby shouted. Harry held the kite up above his head as

Ruby tugged on her plaits for luck.

"Blast off!" she yelled and started to run, holding on to the kite string. Harry let go and the kite bobbed along behind Ruby.

Then a gust of wind caught it. The kite sailed up, up and away. It dipped and swirled, doing gymnastics in the

air. Ruby held on tightly as the wind tugged it higher and higher.

"It's getting away!" Ruby shouted as the string slipped through her fingers.

"Hang on!" Harry called and raced after the kite. The wind blew the kite in wild circles while the cousins chased after it.

"It's heading right for Grandad's

pear tree," Harry said. "It's going to ..." Ruby and Harry both covered their eyes, "... crash!" Harry finished, as their kite collided with the tree.

"Oh, no!" Ruby sighed. She scrambled up the pear tree as quickly as she could.

"The kite's ripped pretty badly," she said, poking her finger through a tear in the paper at the top. She jumped down and handed Harry the kite.

"I'm sure we can fix it," Harry said, sitting down on the grass. He tore a page out of his puzzle book, glued it over the tear and then held up the kite to examine his work.

"Let's fly it again," Ruby said, just as she felt a drop of rain on her nose. For a split second she was disappointed – they couldn't fly their kite in the rain. But then she remembered that rain always brought a magical puppy who took them on amazing adventures.

"Woof! Woof!"

"Puddle!" Ruby and Harry shouted as the puppy bounded across the damp grass towards them.

Puddle barked again as he slipped on the grass and started sliding right in the direction of Harry and the kite!

Chapter Two
Splashtime Surprises

"Watch out!" Ruby called. But it was too late. With a ripping sound, the little puppy skidded right through the colourful kite and rolled on the ground, wrapping himself up in the kite string. He was wriggling so much that when Ruby picked him up he tangled her in the string as well.

"Oh, Puddle!" Ruby giggled. "Can

you try not to be so naughty?"

"We'd just fixed it," Harry said, as he looked through a Puddle-size hole in the kite.

Puddle batted Ruby's plaits as she untangled herself and the puppy from the kite string. He leapt from Ruby's arms. The rain pitter-pattered on the

paving stones as Puddle ran ahead.
He scampered down Grandad's
garden path until he came to a very
large puddle.

The puppy circled it and then dived
in nose first, splashing Ruby and
Harry. His wagging tail disappeared
into the water. Harry wiped flecks of
mud from his glasses. Then he closed
his eyes, held his nose, jumped feet
first into the puddle and disappeared.

Ruby bounced beside the puddle.

"Cannonball!" she cried as she jumped up and held on to her knees. She made a huge splash and then was gone.

When Ruby opened her eyes she couldn't see a thing – not even Puddle or her cousin Harry. Thick, murky fog rolled around her. It was like being trapped in a marshmallow.

"Harry?" Ruby called, reaching out her hand to find him.

"Argh!" Harry jumped as Ruby's hand touched his shoulder.

"It's me," Ruby said. "But where's Puddle?" Then she felt something brush against her. "Puddle, I really

hope that's you."

Puddle's wagging tail thumped against her leg. The fog was so thick she could see the tail but not the puppy. She heard Puddle sniff the air and then his tail disappeared into the fog.

"Hey, come back," Ruby called. "You'll get lost."

"I think we are lost already," Harry added.

"Where do you think we are?" Ruby squinted into the fog. She couldn't see anything.

"Technically we are in a cloud that is making contact with the ground," Harry stated matter-of-factly.

"But where's the cloud?" Ruby asked. She shuffled forward, waving her arms in front of her. "Look, I'm a zombie trapped in clotted cream!"

Harry stayed close to her as a breeze seemed to nudge them forward. He wiped his glasses. "I think the fog is clearing."

Ruby could see a dark shape up ahead. She stumbled forward. "There's something over there." Colours came into focus. "Harry, look! It's green, red and gold with horns and . . ." Ruby stopped and stared. *It couldn't be*, she thought. *It can't be real!*

She could see a long, green scaly body looped round and round, ending in a head nearly as big as she was. Its huge eyes were closed.

"Hey, Ruby, what is it?" Harry shouted from behind her.

"Shhhh," Ruby hissed. She couldn't believe what she was about to say. "It's a . . . it's a . . ." She couldn't get the words out.

"A what?" Harry asked loudly.

Ruby reached over and clapped her hand across Harry's mouth. She whispered, "I think it's a –"

"A dragon!" Harry shouted through Ruby's fingers. "*AAARRRGGGHHH!*"

"Shhhh," Ruby told Harry. "It's sleeping."

They stood rooted to the spot with fear. Ruby heard something – a weird, sniffly snore – coming from the dragon.

"Do you hear that, Harry?" she whispered.

Puddle ran out of the fog and bounded up to the sleeping dragon.

The dragon started to move.

"It's waking up," Ruby said.

Puddle growled at the shuddering creature.

Beginning to back away, Harry spluttered, "Now can I scream for help?"

Chapter Three
Puddle the Brave

Ruby lunged for the puppy but he slipped out of her grasp and barked at the dragon.

"That thing is going to have Puddle for breakfast," Ruby said as the puppy circled the dragon while she chased after him.

"And us for lunch," Harry added.

The dragon's body wriggled and

squirmed. Puddle gently gripped the
dragon's mane in his teeth.

"No, Puddle," Ruby hissed, but she
was too late.

To Ruby's amazement, the dragon

raised its colourful head and spoke.

"Stop that!"

Ruby and Harry gasped and Puddle dived behind their legs. The dragon's head reared back. Ruby covered her ears, expecting it to roar. But instead, a boy's face appeared from under the dragon's head. Ruby rubbed her eyes. She didn't understand what she was seeing.

"You're not a dragon," Harry said. He reached out his hand to help the boy crawl out of the dragon's head. The boy had short black hair and a round face with dimples that looked like they were used to smiling, but his eyes were sad.

Ruby moved closer to the dragon. She could now see that its scales were made of coloured paper and its head was decorated with feathers and glitter.

"Where did you come from?" the boy asked, standing up. "I'm Li."

"My name is Ruby, this is my cousin Harry and that's Puddle," Ruby explained.

A gentle breeze swirled around them, clearing the fog. Now Ruby could see they were surrounded by tall buildings. She noticed that the houses had freshly painted red doors, and there were red and gold lanterns hanging up all along the road.

"Hey," Harry squinted up at the banners draped above their heads. "Those signs are in Chinese."

"Of course. We're in Chinatown," Li said.

The lovely smell of ginger and oranges filled the air. The streets were

starting to fill with people.

"What's going on?" Ruby asked.

Everyone was dressed in brightly

coloured costumes. She could see someone carrying a bunch of balloons, and down the street she thought she spotted a float with a huge paper tiger on it. "It looks like a party."

"The Chinese New Year parade is about to start." Li explained that Chinese New Year is fifteen days of special meals, parades, fireworks and family celebrations.

"I love parades," Ruby piped up. She began to march up and down the street, forming her own parade with Puddle nipping at her heels. Everyone looked happy and excited – everyone except Li.

"What's the matter, Li?" Harry asked when the Ruby and Puddle parade had finished.

"My family and I have just moved here to live with my grandfather. I found his old dragon in the attic, and I wanted to make it dance in the Chinese New Year parade." Li tried to smile. "But I can't do it by myself and I don't know anyone here yet."

Ruby reached down and stroked the dragon's long, glittery mane.

"It would make my grandfather so happy to see me carry on the tradition of the dragon dance," Li continued. "You see, we were both born dragons."

"You're not a real dragon –" Ruby started to say.

"That's not what Li means," Harry corrected. "In China, each year is named after an animal. So you might be born as a monkey or a rat or a pig."

Ruby put her hands on her hips. "I'm not a pig."

"The pig is a very noble animal," Li said, laughing. "But maybe you're a tiger or a horse instead."

"Woof! Woof!" Puddle rolled over in front of Li.

"Yes, or even a dog, Puddle," he added and rubbed Puddle's tummy.

"Hey, maybe we could help you make the dragon dance in the parade,"

Harry suggested.

"I've done ballet dancing," Ruby said, twirling. "I'm sure we could learn to dragon dance."

Li looked at his sleepy dragon and at the crowds starting to gather along the street up ahead. "That's very nice of you, but the parade will start soon. I don't think we'll have time to learn to work together to make the dragon dance."

"Come on, Li," Ruby begged. "Let's at least give it a go."

Puddle pranced about excitedly.

"It's worth a try," Harry added. "What have we got to lose?"

"I suppose it's like my grandfather

49

always says," Li's eyes brightened. "'Do not fear going forward slowly; fear only to stand still.'"

"What?" Ruby gave Li a confused look.

"It means you shouldn't worry if you don't succeed straight away – what's important is that you try," Li explained.

"In other words, get ready to dance like a dragon!" Harry said with a smile.

Chapter Four
A Lucky Charm

"Now, the first thing we need to do is get Lucky up on his feet." Li handed a pole to Harry and one to Ruby. The poles were attached to the dragon's long body.

"The dragon is called Lucky?" Harry asked.

"That's not a very scary name," Ruby said, looking at the dragon's big eyes. "What about Fang or Flame or something really frightening?"

"Chinese dragons aren't scary," Li said. "They are helpful and very wise." He picked up the dragon's head and smoothed the rumpled feathers on its face.

Ruby stroked the feathers. "Wow, these are pretty colours," she said.

"Lucky is mostly green because that's the colour of a good harvest. Gold is for prosperity, and red is for joy," Li said.

"So he's a rich, happy dragon?" Ruby said. "No wonder you called him Lucky."

Ruby and Harry lifted the poles

over their heads. "Now the dragon looks like he's a camel with two humps," Ruby joked. She thought Lucky's horns looked like deer antlers, and his long serpent's body had fishy scales that glistened in the light. "Hey, Lucky looks like all kinds of animals rolled into one. His teeth are just like a tiger's –"

Pounce!

Puddle leapt like a small spotty tiger on to Lucky's tail, which had been twitching in the wind.

"*Tao qi*, Puddle," Li said.

"What did you say?" Harry asked.

"Sorry, it means naughty in Mandarin Chinese," Li said.

"*Tao qi*, Puddle," Ruby repeated.

The puppy nudged the dragon's pointy tail back into place.

"Looks like Puddle wants to help

the dragon dance too." Ruby ruffled Puddle's ears playfully and then smoothed the scales on the dragon's tail.

"Li, you be the head and Puddle can be the tail," Harry suggested, placing the green dragon's tail in Puddle's mouth. Puddle shook his head and set the dragon's tail and his own wagging.

"But how do we dance?" Ruby asked, waving her pole and watching the dragon's long body wiggle in response.

"Just do what I do," Li said, slipping the dragon's head on like a hat.

"Like the game Simon Says," Harry explained to Ruby.

"Or the Hokey Cokey," Ruby said, putting her left foot in and then her left foot out and shaking it all about.

"Let's try it," Li shouted. He showed them how to sway the poles to make Lucky fly and dip the poles to make him swim. It was tricky to get the movements right.

"This is fun!" Ruby called to Harry and Li as she swung the pole back

and forth and watched the dragon
fly over her head. Puddle was
whipped around at the very end of
the dragon. He scampered along,
trying to keep up.

"Let's try a curlicue," Li called as he swept Lucky's head down low and started to make spiralling circles.

"I don't know," Harry protested. He stumbled over his feet, but managed to keep up.

By the time it was Puddle's turn to spin, he hopped and tumbled in the air. He rolled into Ruby, who bumped into Harry, who staggered into Li – and Lucky the dragon tumbled to the ground.

Chapter Five
The Dragon Dance

They all ended up in a pile, laughing. "I'm not sure we're ready," Harry said as he stood up and dusted himself off. "This is harder than it looks."

Boom! Boom! Boom! Boom! Loud drumbeats echoed down the city streets.

"We'll just have to try our best," Li said. "Those drumbeats mean that the parade will start soon."

"Then it's time for this dragon to fly," Ruby said, tugging on her plaits for luck. "Come on!"

Li, Ruby, Harry and Puddle took their places. Lucky swayed above them.

"Now, follow me and we'll get in line for the parade. We'll have to hurry," Li said. He swerved left past a bicycle and then right past a person

carrying shopping. He dipped the
dragon head low to avoid a banner
stretched above the road, and then
leapt up to jump a high kerb. Ruby,
Harry and Puddle followed as fast as
they could.

The drumbeats became faster
and the dragon twisted and turned
as it swam through a sea of people.
When they turned the final corner,
Ruby looked out from under Lucky.

She spotted a long golden dragon heading right for them!

"Li, look out!" she shouted. Li skidded to a halt. The other dragon wobbled but couldn't stop. Li tried to jump out of the way. He dived to the left but Ruby jumped to the right. She heard a terrible ripping sound as the green paper dragon tore apart.

The golden dragon crashed into the pavement between them, its body flipping over the top of Lucky. When Ruby looked up the dragons were twisted together in a coil of green and gold.

Li stood and picked up Lucky's head from the street. "Poor Lucky,"

he said sadly, stroking the dragon's
nose.

"Is everyone OK?" Ruby asked.

Harry groaned. "I'm pretty sure
I'm in one piece, but I don't think
Lucky is."

"Oh, no. Sui, look at our dragon!" said a boy as he crawled out from under the golden dragon.

"I know, Cheng," said a girl, lifting up the golden dragon's crumpled neck. "Goldie is ruined."

"Wait, where's Puddle?" Ruby said, looking around. "Puddle!"

"Puddle! Puddle!" Harry and Li

started looking for Puddle under
layers of torn green and gold paper
and decorations.

Then they heard a muffled bark. It
was coming from the golden dragon's
head in the middle of the pavement.
The huge decorated head was broken
and split. Ruby lifted it up and found
Puddle crouched underneath.

"There you are," she said, lifting the
puppy and hugging him.

"Now Li won't get to dance in the parade to honour his grandfather," Harry whispered to Ruby.

Puddle hopped down and nudged one dragon and then the other. The dragons seemed to shiver together at the puppy's touch.

"Hey, what's your puppy doing?" the girl called Sui asked.

"Naughty, Puddle," Harry scolded, and tried to grab the frisky puppy.

"Puddle's not naughty," Ruby said with a twinkle in her eye. "I think he's got the right idea."

Chapter Six
Go, Team Dragon!

"Let's put the two dragons together and make one ginormous dragon," Ruby suggested.

"The longer the dragon, the more luck it brings," Li said. "If we put the two dragons together we will have the luckiest dragon ever!"

Sui took a closer look at Goldie. "Actually, our dragon's body looks pretty good," she said. "Just a few tears and scrapes."

Ruby and Harry looked at the torn bits of green paper lying on the road.

"I don't think we can fix much of Lucky's body," Harry said, "but his head looks OK."

Ruby could hear that the drums were beating faster, and she could see the crowd lining the street, waving streamers and sparklers.

"Oh, no," said Li. "The parade's about to start. We won't have time to make a new big dragon."

The other children shook their heads. They started to pick up the pieces from their golden dragon and walk slowly away.

"We might if we stop talking and start doing!" Ruby exclaimed.

Goldie's team looked at each other. Puddle barked.

Ruby poked her finger through a hole in the golden dragon's body. It was just about the same size as the

hole Grandad's pear tree put in their kite. "Harry and I know how to fix the dragons. Our Grandad showed us just this morning."

"What are you talking about, Ruby?" Harry asked.

"The kite! If we could fix the paper kite with patches and glue, then we can fix the paper dragons the same way," Ruby said.

"Where are we going to find patches and glue here?" Li asked.

"There is a whole crowd of people waiting to watch the parade," Ruby said. "Someone must have something we can use to patch up the dragons. Come on!"

The children all went out into the crowd and asked everyone what they had with them that might help.

Cheng got a Chinese newspaper, some elastic bands and some chopsticks from a man selling dumplings.

Harry and Sui came back with some rainbow-coloured streamers, scarves and some sparkly hair clips.

Ruby, Li and Puddle ran up to a lady with a poodle and asked for her help. She gave them some tissues,

hairpins and nail varnish from her bag. Everyone was happy to help.

The children worked quickly, reattaching the poles with scarves and elastic bands.

They patched up all the holes and tears with paper and tissue and used clips, pins and nail varnish to stick everything together.

"Wow!" Ruby said when she looked at their work. They had made a beautiful, long, patchwork green and golden dragon with sparkly rainbow and newspaper scales.

"Lucky looks so different," Li said.

"The dragon is Lucky and Goldie now," Cheng said.

"Lucky-Gold!" Ruby said, stroking the lovely new dragon. "The luckiest dragon around!"

Chapter Seven
Lucky-Gold's Dance

"There's just one bit of Lucky-Gold that's not finished," Harry said. "The pole for the tail was too badly damaged. We don't have any way of holding it up."

"Woof! Woof!" Puddle raced back into the crowd and came out dragging a tattered black umbrella.

"Puddle, you naughty puppy. You

can't just grab someone's umbrella,"
Ruby said.

Harry held it up. Holes dotted the
umbrella top. "I don't think anyone
would use this umbrella to keep out
the rain," he said, "but it's perfect for
keeping up a dragon tail. Thanks,
Puddle!"

Harry opened the umbrella and

Ruby and Li placed the tail on top of it. Puddle gripped the umbrella handle in his mouth and held it high.

Li put on Lucky's head and all the kids lined up behind him, lifting the glistening dragon into the air.

"Now we're ready," Ruby said.

"Let's go!"

The cymbals crashed and the drums beat out the rhythm of the dragon dance. Li called out commands like he was leading a game of Simon Says. By the time they started down the parade route they were dancing as one.

"Lucky-Gold tilt left!" he called.

"Lucky-Gold swerve right! Up! Down! Stop and jump!"

A movement led by Li at one end of the dragon rippled down all the way to the dragon's tail. They made the dragon appear to duck and dive through imaginary waves and soar and sway on the currents of air. Ruby thought it must be what a kite feels

like when it's flying through the sky.
As they wove their way through the
crowded streets, Li spotted his family
up ahead.

"I can see my grandfather – there,"
he called out to his team.

Li led Lucky-Gold in a circle
so that it coiled up in front of his
grandfather. Then he bowed the

dragon's head low in respect. Even Puddle lowered the tail to the ground.

Li's grandfather looked at the majestic green and gold dragon in front of him and smiled.

"Li?" he said quietly. "My little dragon has led the dragon dance?"

Li lifted the dragon's head and waved at his grandfather.

"You have made me very proud,"
his grandfather said.

Ruby smiled. They had done it.

"Who are all your new friends?"
Li's grandfather asked. One by one,
Li introduced all the members of
his dragon-dancing team. Each one
raised and waved their pole over their
head and made Lucky-Gold wiggle
as Li said their name.

"Woof! Woof!" Puddle barked and
wagged the dragon's tail.

"And who is this?" Li's grandfather
asked as Puddle dropped the
umbrella that was holding up Lucky-
Gold's tail and galloped over and
sat right in front of him. The puppy

extended his paw and Li's grandfather
gave it a shake.

"This is Puddle," Li said. Puddle
raced from one member of Li's family
to the next, accepting scratches
behind the ears and long strokes on
his wriggling body.

"Puddle reminds me of an old Chinese proverb." Li's grandfather paused and cleared his throat. "Dogs have many friends because they wag their tails, not their tongues."

Ruby laughed and glanced at Li, now surrounded by Sui, Cheng and Goldie's other dancers. Thanks to two tangled dragons, Puddle wasn't the only one with new friends.

Chapter Eight
New Year, New Friends

Li's family clapped and cheered as Li led his team in one final dance. They shouted, "*Xin Nian Kuai Le!*"

"What are they saying?" Ruby asked, dipping her pole down low and then sweeping it upwards.

"Happy New Year," Harry translated. He nudged his glasses back in place.

"Happy New Year, everyone!" Ruby shouted.

The drumbeats rolled to a stop as Lucky-Gold finished his dance.

"Thank you, everyone," Li said as he took off the dragon head. "You were all great!"

"Hey, we should make a Lucky-Gold team for next year's parade too," Cheng said.

"Yeah, he was the best dragon out there," Sui said.

They all started talking excitedly about what they would do next New Year. Ruby tapped Li on the shoulder. "See, Lucky-Gold has brought you good luck," Ruby said.

"He's found you lots of new friends."

"Including you and Harry," Li said, "and of course Puddle."

Puddle padded over to where Li had laid the dragon's head on the ground. He nudged the head with his nose so the dragon's eyes closed again.

"I think Puddle is ready to go home," Harry said.

"I suppose we are too," Ruby said. "I'm glad you got to give your grandfather his surprise, Li."

Puddle wagged his tail excitedly and ran in circles round Ruby and Harry. Everything started to go blurry, as if they were looking at the city through a waterfall.

"Happy New Year, Li!" Ruby shouted.

"*Xin Nian Kuai Le*," Li shouted back.

As the city faded into a watery haze, fireworks rocketed up and exploded into a sparkling shower of colour above them.

"Wow! It's raining shooting stars!" Ruby said. She closed her eyes and

felt the same tingly, spinning feeling
she'd had the last time Puddle
brought them home.

When Ruby opened her eyes the sun
was shining in Grandad's garden.
Puddle pulled at Ruby's dress,
then ran ahead of the cousins and
disappeared behind Grandad's
pear tree.

"Hey, look what Puddle has left."
Harry picked up a glittery green and
gold dragon scale that was just big
enough to patch up the Puddle-size
hole in their kite. Ruby smiled.

"Now we can fly the kite again!"
Harry said.

"Look, there's something else too,"
Ruby said, as she picked up a fortune
cookie and broke it in half.

"What does it say?" Harry asked.

"*You will have good fortune, good friends and many adventures!*" she read.

"I think our fortune's come true already," Harry said.

"I guess it's just our lucky day!" Ruby said.

Can't wait to find out
what Puddle will do next?
Then read on! Here is the first
chapter from Puddle's sixth
adventure, Magic Mayhem ...

Puddle
the naughtiest puppy

Magic Mayhem

"It's time for the magic show to start!"
Ruby announced. Her long plaits
swung to and fro as she waved the
glittery magic wand she'd made out
of a wooden spoon covered in silver
tinsel.

Ruby and her cousin Harry were

sitting on the carpet in the lounge of Grandad's cottage, wearing home-made wizard hats. Ruby had stuck little silver stars all over the dark blue paper cones and they twinkled in the darkened room.

"I'm not ready," Harry told Ruby. He pushed his glasses up his nose. "I have to consult my *Big Book of Magic Tricks*," he said. "And I can't see it properly because you closed the curtains."

"Magic shows always happen in the dark," Ruby said. "Watch me use my Hocus-Pocus Plaits to make Grandad's last biscuit disappear like magic. *Abracadabra!*" Ruby tugged

on her plaits for luck, then waved
her wand so it knocked Harry's
wizard hat down over his glasses. She
popped the biscuit into her mouth.

"*Ta-da!*" Ruby spluttered,
with her mouth full of crumbs.
She pointed to the empty plate.

"That wasn't real magic," Harry
said, as he rearranged his hat. "I'll
show you a real magic trick." He
picked up a marble and a paper cup.
"Watch."

Harry held the paper cup in the
palm of his hand and dropped the
marble inside it. He looked at Ruby
over the top of his glasses. "*Hey
presto!*" he said, waving his free

hand over the paper cup. He turned it upside down.

It was empty. The marble had disappeared!

"That's amazing!" Ruby exclaimed as Harry set the cup back down on the carpet. "How did you do that?"

"I made a hole in the bottom of the cup, just like the book told me to," Harry said. "The marble's still in my hand! The next part of the trick is to make the audience believe I've magicked it somewhere else . . . *Hey presto!*" Harry pretended to pull the marble out of one of Ruby's plaits.

"You're a great magician, Hey Presto Harry!" Ruby giggled. "But magicians are supposed to keep their tricks secret."

All at once, a breeze swirled through the room, making the curtains flap and billow. A little bundle of fur bounded into the lounge, with a joyful, "Woof!"

"Puddle, you're back!" Ruby gasped.

He crashed into them. *Whump!* Harry's hat and paper cup and Ruby's hat and magic wand were sent flying across the carpet.

Ruby scooped up their naughty little puppy friend and gave him an enormous cuddly hug. Puddle's tail wagged as he licked her face.

Harry pulled back the curtains. Raindrops were pitter-pattering against the windows. Ruby and Harry beamed at each other. Whenever it rained, Puddle arrived and they all went on amazing adventures together!

To find out what happens
next, get your copy of
MAGIC MAYHEM today!

Ballet Show Mischief

Go on a beautiful ballet adventure
with Puddle, Ruby and Harry.

The children are
whisked away to a
wonderful ballet
show, but the shy
ballerina has stage
fright. The show
must go on! Will
Puddle be able to
find a solution?

Find out in BALLET SHOW MISCHIEF...

Puddle
the naughtiest puppy

Rainforest Hide and Seek

Have you ever wanted to see a rainforest?

Puddle uses his magic to take Ruby and Harry through a puddle and into an incredible animal adventure. Things keep going missing in the rainforest – can Puddle figure out why?

Find out in RAINFOREST HIDE AND SEEK...

Puddle
the naughtiest puppy

Magic Mayhem

Ruby and Harry are amazed to find themselves in a medieval castle...

...when Puddle takes them on their latest adventure! They meet a magician's apprentice who is in deep trouble. He's lost his spell book. Can Puddle save the day?

Find out in MAGIC MAYHEM...

Puddle
the naughtiest puppy

Pirate Surprise

Can you imagine what it's like to
sail on a pirate ship?

Ruby and Harry find
out – when Puddle
takes them on an
amazing adventure
on the high seas!
Captain Redbeard
has a bad case of the
hiccups! Will Puddle
be able to cure him?

Find out in PIRATE SURPRISE...
Coming soon!

Puddle
the naughtiest puppy

Animal Antics

Join Puddle, Ruby and Harry
at the Safari Rescue Park!

All the animals
have problems they
need to overcome
before they can be
released into the
wild. Will Puddle
be able to help the
monkey who is
afraid of heights?

Find out in ANIMAL ANTICS...
Coming soon!

Training

Hi there! It's us again – Ruby and Harry with our amazing friend Puddle the puppy. Today, we're here with **Dogs Trust** – the UK's largest dog charity – to learn why it's so important to teach dogs to be well behaved.

All dogs enjoy learning – but what they like most of all is learning with their owners! Teaching your dog what is right and wrong and how to behave is also known as "training" your dog. Training your dog is a fantastic way to show your dog how much you care and to spend even more time together!

Just imagine how many things you can teach your dog with just a little patience.

Always remember, Puddle is a magical dog, while real dogs and puppies are living animals who need a lot of care, love and attention.

Training Advice:

• Like all of us, dogs don't like getting things wrong and being told off! Telling them they are good, giving them a friendly stroke or a treat are the best ways to train them.

• Did you know that there are lots of special doggy training schools where dogs can learn to be well behaved? These great doggy schools can also teach you how to behave like a good owner and play with your dog to make sure you are both happy and safe.

• If you have a dog, you might already have been to doggy school — but if not, why not talk about it with your parents?

Congratulations – you have begun to learn about training dogs.

Next time we will be talking about where a dog rests – we can't wait! See you then.

Remember, "A dog is for life, not just for Christmas®"
Dogs Trust has 18 Rehoming Centres around the UK and Ireland. To find out more please go to:
www.dogstrust.org.uk
For more fun and games please go to:
www.learnwithdogs.co.uk

DogsTrust

Ruby Shadows!

Study the picture of Ruby below – she is trying to fly! Can you work out which of the shadows opposite would exactly match the picture?

Mystery Circles!

A piece of a character is shown in
each circle. Look at the clues and see
if you can work out who is shown in
each picture.

**1. I like to pull
my plaits for luck.**

2. I always appear when it rains.

3. I've recently moved to a new town.

4. I'm full of interesting facts.

Answers on the next page

Answers to puzzles:
Ruby Shadows! Shadow C
Mystery Circles! 1. Ruby, 2. Puddle, 3. Li, 4. Harry

For more magical adventures,
come and play with Puddle at

www.puddlethepuppy.com

Use this special code to get
extra-special games and free
stuff at puddlethepuppy.com

COOKIE